William Shakespeare's

Twelfth Night

or

'What You Will'

TEACHER'S RESOURCE BOOK

Philip Page and Marilyn Pettit

ILLUSTRATED BY
Philip Page

Published in association with

Hodder & Stoughton
A MEMBER OF THE HODDER HEADLINE GROUP

Acknowledgements
The publisher would like to thank the following copyright holders for permission to reproduce their photographs:
Pages 49 (left and right), 57 © Alex Bailey Productions Limited
Page 51 © Entertainment in Video
Page 3 © Phil Page
Pages 28, 29, 48 © Royal Shakespeare Company

Every effort has been made to trace copyright holders of material reproduced in this book. Any rights not acknowledged here will be acknowledged in subsequent printings if notice is given to the publisher.

Orders: please contact Bookpoint Ltd, 39 Milton Park, Abingdon, Oxon OX14 4TD. Telephone: (44) 01235 400414, Fax: (44) 01235 400454. Lines are open from 9.00–6.00, Monday to Saturday, with a 24 hour message answering service. Email address: orders@bookpoint.co.uk

British Library Cataloguing in Publication Data
A catalogue record for this title is available from The British Library

ISBN 0 340 74298 4

First published 1999
Impression number   10 9 8 7 6 5 4 3 2 1
Year   2005 2004 2003 2002 2001 2000 1999

Text Copyright © Phil Page and Marilyn Pettit
Illustrations Copyright © 1999 by Phil Page

Cover illustrations by Lee Stinton
Typeset by Fakenham Photosetting Ltd, Fakenham, Norfolk
Printed in Great Britain for Hodder & Stoughton Educational, a division of Hodder Headline Plc, 338 Euston Road, London NW1 3BH by Hobbs the Printers, Totton, Hampshire.

Contents

Introduction

The worksheets in this Teacher's Resource Book are intended to be used with *Livewire Shakespeare: Twelfth Night Pupil's Book*. All references, such as page numbers, relate to that book.

The worksheets address the pupils directly, so that, where appropriate, there is opportunity for pupil autonomy. However, the majority of the tasks lend themselves to teacher/pupil/class interaction.

They attempt to provide a background to Shakespeare and his theatre, so that the play can be viewed as a *stage play*, rather than a text. This approach is continued throughout the book.

All four language modes: Speaking, Listening, Reading and Writing are considered in the tasks.

There are a variety of activities, so that pupils experience: collaborative and individual work; a wide range of written pieces; drama pieces; and debate and discussion with reference to both Shakespearean language and today's English.

The activities have been devised with the SATs and the 'teenage classroom' in mind.

Together with the development of an understanding of Shakespeare, the emphasis is on fun, where pupils learn to support and evaluate their work.

Who was William Shakespeare?

Many people think that Shakespeare is the greatest writer who has ever lived.
That is why you are looking at one of his plays nearly 400 years after he wrote it!

The trouble is, we don't really know very much about him. The sentences below give what are probably the main facts of his life, but they are not in the correct order.

1 Can you write them out in the right order so that they make sense?

5 • He went to London and became an actor sometime in the 1580s.

2 • When he was about seven years old he went to Stratford Grammar School.

1 • William Shakespeare was born in Stratford-upon-Avon in Warwickshire in 1564.

6 • Before he died, he wrote 37 plays and lots of poetry.

3 • He left school at 14 and got married to Anne Hathaway in 1582.

7 • He died at the age of 52 and was buried in his home town of Stratford.

4 • They had three children: Susanna, Hamnet and Judith.

2 Work out the answers to these questions:

In which year did he first go to school?

How old was he when he got married?

In which year did he die?

Every picture tells a story

What do you think this title means?

1 Discuss this with a partner and then report back to your class.
What did you come up with?

It might mean: when you look at a picture or a photograph, there is more to it than you think!
It might mean: when you see something going on, there is more happening than you think!

2 Look at the picture on the front cover of *Twelfth Night*. What can you see? Two faces, a tankard that might hold ale (beer), and wedding rings!
Try to come up with answers to these questions:

- Do you think the faces are happy or sad?
- What might the tankard tell you that some of the characters like doing?
- What about the rings? How many weddings do you think there will be?

Did you say that:
– some of the characters will like drinking and being happy!
– weddings are happy times especially if there are three!?

Did you wonder why the faces look so worried?

You know that *Twelfth Night* is a comedy. That means even if the characters are worried, everything will turn out fine in the end.

Let's collect the clues!
Two sad people; three weddings; lots of drinking!
Celebrations!
Perhaps they won't be sad after all then . . .
Perhaps they'll end up going to a few weddings . . .
Perhaps they'll have a party . . .
Perhaps we ought to read it and find out . . .

Shakespeare's theatre

1 Look at the photograph of the stage of the Globe Theatre. Can you see any differences between this stage and the ones you see today?

There are lots of things missing:

- NO curtains at the front
- NO scenery
- NO loudspeakers
- NO sides to the stage
- NO lighting
- NO props (things put on stage to set a scene.)

2 What problems would this cause Shakespeare? To help you work this out, think of the solutions to these problems:

- With no curtains can everyone die on stage? If not, what has to happen?
- With no curtain, how might we tell that a scene has ended?
- With no sides to the stage, how do the actors go offstage?
- With no sides to the stage, isn't the audience close? What might this mean for the actors?
- With no props, how can the audience tell where a scene is set?
- With no lighting, how does the audience know what time it is in the play?
- With no lighting, when can the plays take place?
- With no loudspeakers or electrical equipment, how can sound effects, like thunder storms be put across?

The groundling's experience!

Imagine standing in the middle of a theatre in Shakespeare's time!
STANDING all the way through a play! Standing in the middle of a crowd! Standing for over TWO hours!
Bet you can't imagine it ... yet!

Now picture what it *might* have been like:

- no seats
- no toilets
- no deodorants
- no rubbish bins.

SMELLY and SWEATY!
The floor was covered in hazel nut shells. Bet that didn't help take the smells away!
The crowd could move around. At least they could walk out of the boring bits!
The crowd could shout at the actors. Bet the actors were worried in case the crowd didn't like them!
The crowd could talk. Bet it was really noisy!
There was no roof! Oh no, what if it rained? SMELLY, SWEATY AND WET!
What if the sun came out again? SMELLY, SWEATY, WET AND STEAMING!
No wonder the groundlings were called penny *stink*ards!
Some rich people could sit on the stage or behind it. Bet the crowd talked about them and their clothes!

In fact, it was very different from today wasn't it?

1 If you've been to the theatre, write down how you are expected to behave. Write down what the inside of the theatre looks like.

2 Imagine you're a groundling. Write about a time you went to see a play.
Use the information above to help you describe that day.

Cast of characters

Even before you begin reading the play, you will need to look at the **cast of characters** on pages iv–v.

1 Look at the drawings of each character. Read the words underneath them, because these words tell you something about each character. They will help you form your *first impressions*.

You are lucky. At least you can read about them. An audience would just have to sit down or stand and wait for the characters to show themselves on stage, before they could decide.

2 Now ... just think ... if you had to choose TWO of these characters to spend an afternoon with, just talking and enjoying yourself, which TWO would you pick? Write down the reasons for your choices.

3 Then again ... which TWO characters would you definitely NOT want to spend any time with?
Write down the reasons for your choices.

Share these ideas with a partner and see if you came up with the same characters.

Reported scenes

Just think how long a play would be if the audience had to watch everything that happened. We would get very tired, perhaps even bored.

That's why Shakespeare made sure that his actors **reported** some of the action.

Now here's your chance to try writing your own Shakespeare scene!

1 Look again at page 1. The messenger has to **report** to Orsino exactly what Olivia's handmaid has told him.
Using his lines, and then more of your own, write down the conversation that might have taken place between the messenger and the handmaid.

The first few lines have been done:

Messenger: I have come to speak to your mistress, Countess Olivia.

Handmaid: Who sent you?

Messenger: The Duke Orsino.

2 When you have finished, work with a partner, and read or act your scene out to the rest of your group.

- What did they think of your work?
- If you listened to other pupils' scenes, what did you think of theirs?

When you give your opinion of other work, or when you listen to what other people think of your work – you are **evaluating** work.

An eyewitness account

An **eyewitness account** is told by a person who has really seen something happen, not just heard about it from someone else. That means that he or she can tell you *exactly* what went on and how he or she felt as things happened.

Look at page 2. Poor Viola has been shipwrecked.

Imagine that you live in Illyria. You are walking along the cliffs when suddenly you see a ship in trouble. You stop and watch everything that happens, even Viola being washed ashore.

You rush home to tell your family what you have seen. You want to give them **an eyewitness account** of the shipwreck.

Use the drawing on page 2 to help you describe what you saw.

You might begin:

Mum, Dad, you'll never guess what I've just seen. I was out near the beach, when all of a sudden . . .

Remember reported scenes?

We never see Viola and the Captain persuading Orsino to take her on as a servant, do we?

- We know that Viola has disguised herself as a man.
- We know that she is calling herself Cesario.

What we don't know is how she managed to get work with Orsino.

Try to report this scene using a storyboard.
It has already been drawn out. All you have to do is draw the pictures that go in each frame and add the text (words) that the characters say.

1	2	3
4	5	6

Working with a partner in role

When you're **in role**, you pretend to be someone else. You play act.

You take on a role and try to say what you think that person would say ... you **improvise**.

1 Look at page 4. This tells us that Maria is passing on a message from Olivia. Olivia is cross with Sir Toby because he is drunk and comes in late.

2 With a partner, **improvise** the scene between Maria and Olivia. Olivia is telling Maria what she should say to Sir Toby and how she feels about the way Sir Toby is behaving. Use your own words as much as possible but here are some clues to help you:

- 'What a plague means my niece to take the death of her brother thus?'
- 'my lady takes great exceptions to your ill hours'
- 'you must confine yourself within the modest limits of order'
- 'That quaffing and drinking will undo you'

You can add as much as you like to your **role play**.

3 When you have finished, show it to another pair and listen to their opinion of your scene.

4 Listen to theirs and decide what was different and what was the same.

5 Together, in a group of four, talk about why you came up with certain ideas.
Remember that this is called **evaluating** your own work.

What's he like?

Shakespeare often tells us about a character before that person appears on stage.

When we arc in the audience, this gives us the chance to hear about characters before we see them. We find out what others think of them.

1 Look at pages 4 and 5. Maria and Sir Toby talk about Sir Toby's friend Sir Andrew Aguecheek.
Read what they have to say again on those pages.

2 Now imagine that you have been asked to describe Sir Andrew. Write down what you might say about him.

Here are some clues to help you:

- 'a foolish knight'
- 'He's as tall a man as any's in Illyria'
- 'he has three thousand ducats a year'
- 'a very fool and a prodigal'
- 'he plays o' th' viol-de-gamboys, and speaks three or four languages word for word without book, and hath all the good gifts of nature'
- 'he hath the gift of a coward'
- 'he would quickly have the gift of a grave'

First impressions

You have used the **evidence** from pages 4 and 5 to help you describe Sir Andrew.
This **evidence** was based on what Sir Toby, Maria and others said about him.
What they said gave you your **first impressions** of Sir Andrew.
Not everything people say about someone is true, is it?

1 Look at pages 6 and 7.
Read them again and decide what Sir Andrew is really like!

2 Present your **evidence** to a partner. You will need to make notes. Be prepared to explain these to a partner.

The following might help you:

- He calls Maria a 'shrew' when he first meets her. How do you think Maria will take that?
- What mistake does he make with Maria's name a bit further on in the cartoon?
- Apart from making a mistake with her name, he says, 'I desire better acquaintance'. How does this annoy Maria?
- How can you tell he gives up on things easily?
- How does he want to spend his time?

Act I: Scene 4

1 Look at the Key Scene on page 8.

2 Answer the questions below, by reading the text carefully. You will need to write your answers in full sentences.

- What tells you that Orsino really trusts Cesario/Viola?
- Can you put 'address thy gait unto her' into your own words?
- Who is 'her' in that line?
- How does Orsino tell Cesario to behave when he arrives at Olivia's doors?
- Can you remember what Olivia's 'sorrow' is?
- Why does Orsino think that his messages of love will seem better coming from Cesario?
- There is a clue in the last line spoken by Cesario that tells us how Cesario feels towards Orsino. Can you decide how Cesario feels?
- The last line is an *aside*. That means that it is spoken out to the audience. No character on stage hears it. How do you think the audience feels for Cesario now that they have heard this aside?

Let's sit down and have a chat, shall we? Who me? I'm not one to gossip . . .

Everybody **chats** and **gossips** about other people.
Sometimes, it can be mean, but most of the time, it doesn't do any harm.
Characters **chat** and **gossip** in Shakespeare's plays.

1 Look at page 8. Orsino is giving Cesario (Viola) instructions about what to say to Olivia. Have you noticed how many people are on stage at this point?
Here's a clue:

The Duke tells Cesario to go and … 'some four or five attend him – All, if you will; for I myself am best when least in company.'

2 Imagine that some of these people go off to another room and **gossip** about the Duke and his love for Olivia.
What might they say?

3 In a group of four, write down some ideas first. When you have enough, write the script of the conversation that might take place.
Here are some questions to help you get started:

- What does the Duke do all day?
- What does that mean his servants have to do all day?
- Does he stand a chance with Olivia?
- Why doesn't he stand a chance?
- Will the Duke's servants like this new boy Cesario much?
- Will they think that Cesario stands a chance of seeing Olivia?
- Could the servants be a bit fed up of the Duke?

When you have finished your written work, you could read it out to other groups.

A speech of love

Look again at page 14.

Olivia says: 'Where lies your text?'

This tells us that Cesario has prepared a speech to recite to Olivia.

When Cesario asks to see Olivia's face, Olivia says: '**You are now out of your text**'. This was not part of the speech. In fact, Cesario never manages to recite the prepared speech.

1 Imagine that you are Cesario, trying to make Olivia love Orsino, your master.

2 Write the speech that you would recite to Olivia.

REMEMBER:

- make her feel good about herself
- make her feel happy
- say how beautiful she looks
- talk about her lovely clothes
- mention her voice, her eyes, her hair

In all of this, you must **flatter** Olivia.

Act I: Scene 5

You might have already tried to write a speech of love. Now you are going to work out a few more facts from a closer study of the words.

1   Answer the following in full sentences.

- Olivia takes off her veil and pretends that her face is a painting. Can you try to describe the way she looks from the words: you might think of her lips and her eyes, and then use the cartoons to help you.
- What has Olivia heard about Orsino's character? You will need to read her words and put them into today's English.
- Look at what Cesario tells Olivia he would do if he loved her. Can you put these words in today's English?
- What Cesario says he would do sounds rather silly to us, don't you think? What would you have said if Olivia had asked you 'Why, what would you?'

2   Once you have answered these questions, share your answers with a partner.

Did you end up saying the same things? If not, try to decide whose words in today's English sound the best.

Can you mind read?

To work out what someone else might be thinking and to understand how someone else might be feeling, we often try to collect **evidence**.

Evidence could be:

- the way someone behaves and acts
- the way that person moves his/her body
- the words that person uses
- the way in which the words are spoken

You are going to try to work out what Olivia is thinking and how she is feeling.

1 Read page 16 again. This is where Olivia pretends that Cesario has left a ring and that she doesn't want it. She sends Malvolio after Cesario to return the ring.

2 Put yourself in Olivia's place and try to write down what she is thinking and how she is feeling, now that Malvolio has left with the ring.

You might begin:

'Oh no, have I done the right thing? Should I have sent Malvolio after the boy? I feel so . . .

Can you predict the future?

Not many people believe that we can see into the future. There are times in Shakespeare's plays though, when the audience can see what is going to happen, but the characters can't.

1 Look at page 17: Act 2: Scene 1.
Read the scene again.

- It tells us that Sebastian is alive
- He has been staying with Antonio
- He is leaving Antonio's house
- Now he is off to travel around Illyria
- He was saved by Antonio from the sea
- He thinks that Viola, his sister, is drowned
- He is off to Duke Orsino's house
- Antonio is not a friend of Orsino
- Antonio will go after Sebastian.

2 Can you find the lines that give us each of those pieces of information?
These are facts.
Now try to predict the future ...

3 Using the following clues, try to say what you think might happen in the future:

- My name is Sebastian
- It was said she much resembled me
- She is drowned already
- I am bound to the Count Orsino's court
- I have many enemies in Orsino's court
- I do adore thee so ... I will go.

Reading someone's mind

Remember when Olivia sent Malvolio after Cesario? She pretended that Cesario had left a ring and that she didn't want it.

This time look at Act 2: Scene 2 on page 18.
Malvolio has found Cesario and he has returned the ring. Of course, the audience knows that Cesario didn't leave a ring!

Try to put yourself in Cesario's place and then write down what you are thinking.
You can use the text (the words) to help you, but try to use your own words as much as possible.

Here are some words from the text to help you:

- Fortune forbid my outside have not charm'd her!
- her eyes had lost her tongue
- she did speak in starts
- She loves me, sure
- Disguise, I see thou art a wickedness
- What will become of this?
- My state is desperate for my master's love
- time, thou must untangle this

You might use the ideas above and perhaps start with the words:

'A ring? What's this? I didn't give her a ring … Oh no! …

How we might describe people

When we describe a person, we use **adjectives**.

Look at pages 19 and 20.
You are going to try to describe Maria, Sir Andrew and Malvolio.

1 Read all the **adjectives** below and try to match them up with the right character.
You might use one **adjective** to describe more than one character.
Use a dictionary to help you work out the meanings.

> cross   annoyed   clever   mischievous   devious
> drunk   patient   happy   loyal   rude

Now look at Sir Toby in this scene.

2 Choose five **adjectives** that describe him. Once you have written them down, put each one in a sentence.
If you decide that Sir Toby is **funny**, you might write:

When Sir Toby is drunk on stage and he sings with the Clown, I think the audience would think he was funny.

Problem pages

There are problem pages in many magazines and newspapers. When someone is worried about something they write to the magazine asking for advice. The person who answers these letters is called an agony aunt.

These are the letters that Orsino, Viola and Olivia have written to a magazine.

You are the agony aunt, and you need to write back and give them some advice.

Dear ...

I am so fed up. I'm in love with a beautiful woman, called Olivia. I send her flowers, messages of love, rings, but she won't even see my messenger. She sends him back to me, saying that she can never love me. Oh what can I do? I think I will die of a broken heart if she doesn't change her mind.

Dear ...

What am I going to do? I am in terrible trouble. You see, I have disguised myself as a man to get a job in a strange country. The thing is, I am in love with the man I work for, but he loves another. This is all so mixed up. Should I tell him I'm really a woman and risk making him angry? Or should I keep up the disguise and hope everything will turn out well in the end?

Dear ...

There is a man who lives close to me who keeps sending messages saying he loves me. I can never love him, but I have realised that I love his servant, the messenger boy? I don't know what to do for the best? Should I tell this boy how I feel or keep quiet and hope?

Writing a challenge!

When you are really angry with someone, you might argue with that person. You might even end up shouting.

1 Write about a time when you were really cross with someone. Can you remember why you were angry? What did you say and what did you do? What did the other person say and do? How did you make it up at the end?

2 Look again at page 19.
Sir Andrew is really angry with Malvolio.
Can you remember why? Write down the reasons for his anger.

At that time, men **challenged** each other to duels when they were angry or insulted by someone.
Sir Toby, who loves to play tricks, tells Sir Andrew that he will write a **challenge** to Malvolio for Sir Andrew.

3 Imagine that you are Sir Toby. Try to write the **challenge** he will write for Sir Andrew.
Remember that you will have to write:

- why Sir Andrew wants to fight him
- where he wants to fight him
- when he wants to fight him
- what he wants to fight him with – if you look carefully at some of the cartoons where Sir Toby and Sir Andrew are outside in the garden you will see the kind of weapons that might be used!

You might want to begin with the words:

Sir Andrew is so fed up of your rude behaviour that he wants to teach you a lesson. He has decided to ...

Writing a love letter to get revenge!

Do you remember when Cesario tried to tell Olivia how much Orsino loved her?
Cesario was really trying to make Olivia believe him, because he was telling the truth.

1 Now look at Maria's plan on page 20 where she tells Sir Toby that she is going to forge a letter. This letter will be to Malvolio and it will look as if it's from Olivia.
This letter is not telling the truth.
Maria is going to make Malvolio look a fool.

2 Before you read parts of the letter that Malvolio finds, try to write the letter yourself. Remind yourself of what Malvolio is like: miserable, mean, big-headed and he always dresses in boring clothes, in dark colours!
So ...
You might want to make Malvolio look foolish by:

● telling him to act in a silly way
● making him dress in a silly way
● telling him to do daft things with his face.

The audience knows ... but Orsino doesn't

There are many times when we know things that the characters don't.

1 Look again at pages 21 and 22.
How are we made to feel sorry for Viola? We know that she is in love with Orsino and we know that she cannot tell him, because she is supposed to be a boy and in any case, he loves Olivia.

This might help you:

'thine eye hath stay'd upon some favour that it loves'

● Who is the favour?

'What kind of woman is it?'

● It's not a woman. Who is it?

'What years?' 'About your years, my lord'

● How old is this person supposed to be? Who is it really?

'Let still the woman take an elder than herself'

● Orsino tells Cesario that he should marry a younger woman, because women should marry older men. Cesario wants an older man – who is it?

2 Write down your reasons for feeling sorry for Cesario in this scene. Write down what the audience knows but Orsino doesn't.

Act 2: Scene 4

In this scene on page 23 Cesario and Orsino talk about how men and women love, and then Orsino sends Cesario off to see Olivia again.

This is a sad scene for Cesario because, as Viola, she really loves Orsino, and the only way she can tell him is by making up a story about another girl!

1 See if you can write the story of this 'other girl'.
You will need some clues to help you as you are reading the text.

- My father had a daughter lov'd a man
- she never told her love, but let concealment like a worm i' th' bud feed on her damask cheek
- she pin'd in thought
- she sat like Patience on a monument smiling at grief.

When Orsino asks if this girl died, Cesario says that she doesn't know.
NOW you are ready to tell the story of the girl!

2 When you have done this, write down the reasons why you feel sorry for Cesario in this scene.

All of this scene shows us **dramatic irony** – those two words mean that we know what is going on, but Orsino doesn't.

Malvolio's BIG mistake!

Have you noticed that there are people who make lots of mistakes in this play?
Olivia thinks Viola is a man – BIG MISTAKE!
Orsino thinks Viola is a man – another BIG MISTAKE!
Viola thinks Sebastian is dead – BIG MISTAKE!
Sebastian thinks Viola is dead – another BIG MISTAKE!

Malvolio also makes a BIG MISTAKE!
He really believes that Olivia loves him. He doesn't realise that he has been tricked and that the letter is forged.

Decide what Malvolio thinks of himself and what others think of him.

He thinks he is:

_____
_____
_____
_____
_____
_____
_____

Others think he is:

_____
_____
_____
_____
_____
_____
_____

What do **you** think of him?

Directing a comic scene

Look at Act 2: Scene 5 on page 25.
This is one of the funniest scenes in the play.
You have already worked out what **you** think of Malvolio, what **others** think of Malvolio and what **he** thinks of himself!

1 In groups of five, you are going to act out and direct the scene.

The first thing to do is:
Read the scene again.

Second:
Give out parts – you will need parts for: Malvolio, Sir Toby, Fabian and Sir Andrew
The fifth person in your group will be the director.

Third:
You will need to read your parts again and then decide how you're going to act on stage.

Fourth:
You will all have to stand up, and read out parts while **moving around in your space**, remembering to **move your hands and your bodies** to make people laugh!

Remember that Malvolio will be really 'stuck-up', while Sir Toby will be angry. Sir Andrew will be acting foolishly, and Fabian will be trying to keep Sir Toby calm. Those last three will be hiding behind the hedge!

2 Once you have acted it out and decided what you want to do on stage, act it out to the rest of your class and see what they think of it!
The more they laugh, the better your scene will be!

Men and their motives

There are three men who want to marry Olivia!
They are Duke Orsino, Sir Andrew Aguecheek and
Malvolio.

Here are some facts about Olivia:
She is beautiful – look at page 15 and find the line that tells
you that.
She is rich – how do you know?
She is in mourning for her dead brother – look at page 4 and
find the words that tell you that!

The three men have **motives** for marrying Olivia. That
means they have reasons for marrying Olivia.

By thinking of what you have read: try to find out the
motives for each one of the men wanting to marry her.
Like a good detective you must also provide the *evidence*
that backs up what you say.
This might be your **opinion**, but it could also be **lines from
the play**.

Duke Orsino's motives	Sir Andrew's motives	Malvolio's motives

Having a good laugh!

The characters in the picture are having a good laugh.

These actors took the parts of Fabian, Sir Toby Belch and Sir Andrew Aguecheek in a performance of *Twelfth Night*.

Can you spot who is who?

They might just have seen Malvolio in his ridiculous outfit! They might also have been told by Olivia that they will have to look after him because she thinks he is mad.

Try to write the conversation that is taking place between the three characters in this picture.
It should be written in a script, with *stage directions*.
Stage directions are written in *italics* and are often written inside brackets.
They tell the actors how to behave, say words, and move about.

You might start off like this:

Sir Toby: Well, did you ever see such a sight? He looked really stupid dressed like that! (*laughing as he speaks*)

It's Olivia's turn now

When we read Act 3: Scene 1, we have to feel sorry for Olivia. We have already felt sorry for Viola because she has fallen in love with Orsino. Now it's Olivia's turn!

1 Look at the scene (pages 30 and 31) again in pairs. Imagine that you have been asked to write the scene in Modern English; that is English that most people today will understand.

2 You will need to translate the conversation between Olivia and Cesario. This doesn't mean that you have to translate every word, but make sure that the meaning of the scene comes across and that we feel sorry for Olivia.

The first part is done for you:

Olivia: Let me speak a minute. After you left last time, I sent my servant after you, to return a ring. But really it wasn't your ring – you hadn't given me one had you? Oh dear, what must you think of me?

3 Read your scene to another teacher who does not know the play and ask him or her what it was about and what they think happened before it.
This is a good way of testing if you have made a really good job of putting the text into Modern English!

If you could wish for ...

We all wish for things ... we all have our dreams.

1 Ask your friends or your family what they wish for. Perhaps it's a holiday in the sun; lots of money; a big car; good health.

2 Share what you have found out with your partner. Did you find that people wish and dream for similar things?

Look at the characters in *Twelfth Night*.

- Malvolio wishes he could marry Olivia and tell Sir Toby what he thinks of him.
- Sir Andrew dreams of being a brave knight and marrying Olivia.

3 Try to fill in the rest:

- Sir Toby wishes he was ...
- Viola wishes she was ...
- Olivia dreams of being ...
- Orsino wishes he could ...

4 If you could wish for something special, what would it be? Write down what you would wish for and then share that with your partner.

Sir Andrew's letter to Cesario, challenging him to a duel

1 Read the letter below. There are some words missing, but you will be able to fill them in by thinking about what you already know of the play.
Remember that Sir Andrew is a foolish knight, so he wouldn't write very well.

To the Count's serving-man!

I would like to challenge you to a d___. I have decided to fight you, because I saw you with O_____. I am very a____ and I am going to hurt you in e____ places! You had better r__ away or stand and f____, because I love Olivia and I think you are trying to make me j_____.

My friends Sir T___ and Captain F_____ told me that anyway!

Yours, Sir Andrew

Not much of a letter is it?
Could you do better if you wanted to make someone angry enough to fight?

2 Try to write a letter that shows real jealousy and anger.

3 Once you have done that, practise reading it out in a really loud voice that sounds frightening.

4 When you are ready, read it to the class or to a partner. Let them decide what they think of your threat.

Sir Toby has fun with Sir Andrew and Cesario

1 Read pages 39 and 40 again.
This is where Sir Toby tells Cesario how brave Sir Andrew is and then he tells Sir Andrew how brave Cesario is!

2 Write down in your own words how Sir Toby describes Sir Andrew and then Cesario!

Sir Andrew is ...
Cesario is ...

3 Look at what Cesario says:

'I have heard of some kind of men that put quarrels purposely on others to taste their valour'

Who could Cesario be talking about here?

4 What do you think of Sir Toby, now that you have seen what he is up to? Is he still such a funny character? Are you hoping that he will get found out soon and be punished?

One happy; one sad

Read pages 42 and 43 again.

Cesario must be happy – he hasn't had to fight after all and perhaps Sebastian is alive. Antonio must be sad – he has just been arrested and the person he thought was his friend has pretended not to know him and has refused to give him his money. This would make the news in Illyria.

Imagine:

- a duel!
- a young boy saved by Antonio, an enemy!
- the arrest of Antonio, an enemy of Illyria's Duke Orsino!
- a young boy saying that he has never seen Antonio before!

This could be a BIG news story! A SCOOP for the *Illyria Express*!

Try to write the newspaper report of what happened from the time that Antonio burst in to save Cesario to the time when Antonio is taken away by the soldiers.

You will need to look at newspapers to help you with the layout – headlines, columns etc.

You will also have to think about the way you will write the article –

- who did what?
- where did it happen?
- when did it happen?
- why did it happen?

Can you guess who I am?

- I like music.
- I enjoy a good joke.
- I'm not very brave.

So far, I could be Sir Toby, Sir Andrew, perhaps even the Clown. Keep going ...

- I am male.
- I like dancing.
- I can sing a bit as well.

Well? I could still be Sir Toby, Sir Andrew, perhaps even the Clown.
Keep going ...

- I can be found in Olivia's house.

I could still be Sir Toby, Sir Andrew, perhaps even the Clown.
Now for the clue that lets you know exactly who I am ...

- I'm Olivia's uncle.

That's right ... no-one else but Sir Toby.

1 Now choose a character and prepare ten things you could say about him or her.

2 Play this guessing game in pairs. Remember that you want to keep your partner guessing for as long as possible.

Viola/Cesario

In the box below are some words and phrases to describe Viola.

1 Use a dictionary to help you with the words you do not understand.

2 Once you have read them, try to fit them into the grid below. Some letters have already been put in to help you.

> girl   loyal   in disguise   loves Orsino   isn't jealous
> cannot fight   kind   generous   brave   proud

3 When you have done the crossword, give examples from the play that prove that each of those words or phrases is true. For example:

Girl: We know that Viola is a girl because she has a girl's name and she is Sebastian's sister.

Mistakes and their consequences

Read pages 45 and 46.
There are so many mistakes made in these scenes.
The mistakes are written below for you.

1 Write down what the **consequences** of the mistakes are.
Consequences are the things that happen because mistakes
have been made.

- The Clown thinks that Sebastian is really Cesario.
That means that . . .
- Sir Andrew thinks that Sebastian is really Cesario.
So Sir Andrew will . . .
- Sir Toby thinks that Sebastian is really Cesario.
So he will . . .
- Olivia thinks that Sebastian is really Cesario.
She will take him away and . . .

2 How do you think Sebastian feels in all of this?
When Olivia arrives, he might be feeling a bit happier. Why
might that be?

Soliloquies

These are words spoken by the actor to the audience, when there is no-one else on the stage.

They are really useful, because the audience learns the character's thoughts about what has happened and what might happen. The audience also learns about any worries the character might have.

In Act 4: Scene 3 Sebastian is alone on stage for a while before Olivia comes in.

1 Read the scene again and find out all the things that are worrying Sebastian right now!

2 Write them down in sentences.
Here are some lines that might give you clues:

- 'This pearl she gave me, I do feel't, and see't, And though 'tis wonder that enwraps me thus, yet 'tis not madness'
- 'Where's Antonio then?'
- 'His counsel now might do me golden service'
- 'this may be some error'
- 'I am ready to distrust mine eyes'
- 'I am mad, or else the lady's mad'.

3 Now try to find words in the text that Sebastian says to try to stop himself worrying. Write them down in sentences. Here are some clues.

- 'This pearl she gave me, I do feel 't'
- 'I could not find him at the Elephant, yet there he was, and there I found this credit'
- 'the lady's mad; yet if 'twere so, she could not sway her house, command her followers'.

How does the Clown make you laugh?

Making people laugh is really hard. Sometimes jokes that were funny in Shakespeare's time are not at all funny now. You are going to try to find all the jokes and tricks that the Clown plays on characters in *Twelfth Night*, and then you can decide whether you think he is funny or not!

Start with page 10.

- What does he mean when he says 'many a good hanging prevents a bad marriage'?
- How does he prove that Olivia is a fool and not him?

Now move to page 28.

- How does he try to be funny in his answer to Cesario when she says: 'Dost thou live by the tabor?'
- How does he explain that he is not a churchman, but lives by the church?

What about page 45?

- Why does he say – 'No I do not know you, nor I am not sent to you by my lady to bid you come speak with her'?
- Why does he say the opposite of what he really means?
- Does 'nor this is not my nose neither' make you laugh?

Look at what he does on page 47.

- Do you think an audience would find his disguise funny?
- What does he mean when he says 'Then you are mad indeed if you be no better in your wits than a fool'?

So, after following the Clown, what do you think? Is he funny? Did he make you laugh? Look at your answers again, and tell your partner what you think of the Clown now.

Staging a dramatic scene

Look again at Act 5: Scene 1 on page 52.
Orsino is really cross with Olivia, because she cannot love him. Olivia is really cross with Cesario, because she thinks he is her husband and she thinks he should be with her and not with Orsino. She tells Orsino about their marriage!

1 Act out this scene in groups of five.
First – decide on parts. You will need Orsino, Olivia, Cesario, Priest and one Attendant.
Next – read the scene a few times so that you understand what is being said.
These are some things you will need to think about:

- Orsino is very angry, so angry that he is threatening to kill Cesario! You will have to make his voice very loud at times.

- What do you think Orsino will do on the words: 'But hear me this'?

- How can you show Orsino being violent towards Cesario when he says: 'Come, boy, with me; my thoughts are ripe in mischief'?

- What will Olivia do when Cesario tells her that he will follow Orsino because he loves him?

- Try to make the word 'husband' really stand out when Olivia first says it. You will have to make Orsino and Cesario act in a very surprised way.

- What will Cesario be doing as he says: 'No, my lord, not I'? How will Cesario be moving while the Priest says that they are married?

2 When you have decided how you will perform the scene, act it out to a group or your whole class.

What did they think of your performance?

Act 5: Scene 1

Look again at page 55.

1 Make sure that you can answer these questions about the text:

- What do you think everyone is thinking when Sebastian appears on stage?
- Why does Olivia look at Sebastian strangely? Is it because she is cross with him for hitting her uncle?
- How do Sebastian and Viola check that they are really brother and sister?
- Have you noticed that while Sebastian and Viola are checking each other out, no-one else speaks – what do you think they are doing on the stage?
- What is the Captain, who helped Viola at the beginning, busy doing now?
- With the mention of Malvolio's name, what have we been reminded of?

2 Are you happy now that Olivia has Sebastian and Viola has Orsino?
What do you want to happen to Malvolio?

Happy ever after?

At the end of the play there are three happy couples:

. . . are married

. . . are married

. . . are going to
get married

But Malvolio has been tricked. He hasn't got his woman!
Orsino sends Fabian after him to bring him back.
What do you think they say to each other?

Draw a storyboard to show what happens.
Remember that things must end happily in a Shakespearean
comedy.

1 Fabian goes after Mavolio.	2	3
4	5	6 Malvolio agrees to come back.

Now that you've reached the end of the play . . .

Right at the beginning of the play, even before you had started to read it, you decided on the two characters you would most like to spend time chatting with.
You did this by looking at the **cast of characters**.

Now that you've read all the play and learned a lot more about all the characters, have you changed your mind?

- If you have, write down the **two** characters you would most like to spend time with – again, give reasons for your answers.
- If your choice of characters has stayed the same, write down what other things you have learned about them? You might manage to write about five to ten other points.

Character 1	Character 2

Quiz challenge 1

Here's a chance to test your memory and see how good a Shakespearean scholar you really are!
Read the questions, answer them and total your score.

1 When Orsino was desperate to gain Olivia's love, did he:
   a. send her flowers?
   b. send her a letter?
   c. send a messenger to tell her how much he loved her?

2 When Orsino was talking to Cesario about how to behave when he reached Olivia's door, did he tell him to:
   a. break down the door?
   b. stand there with his foot in the door and refuse to leave?
   c. yell and shout and make lots of noise?

3 When Olivia sent Malvolio after Cesario, did she send him with:
   a. a ring?
   b. a letter?
   c. a handkerchief?

4 When Sir Toby, Sir Andrew, Maria and Fabian were spying on Malvolio, did they hide?
   a. behind a garden seat?
   b. up trees?
   c. behind a hedge?

5 Where does the Clown tell Cesario that he lives? Is it:
   a. by the Elephant Inn?
   b. by the church?
   c. by Orsino's house?

6 When Cesario and Sir Andrew fight, who comes to the rescue? Is it:
   a. a policeman?
   b. Sir Toby Belch?
   c. Antonio?

(Continued on Sheet 2)

Quiz challenge 2

(Continued from Sheet 1)

7 Who does the Clown dress up as when he talks to Malvolio in the dark room? Is it:
  a. a priest called Sir Topas?
  b. Olivia?
  c. a doctor?

8 What present does Olivia give to Sebastian? Is it:
  a. a race horse?
  b. a pearl?
  c. a new house?

9 What does Orsino threaten to do when he finds out Olivia loves Cesario?
  a. say he'll kill himself?
  b. say he'll kill Olivia?
  c. say he'll kill Cesario?

10 Who has Viola's clothes – the ones she wore as a girl, before she disguised herself as a boy? Is it:
  a. Malvolio?
  b. the captain?
  c. a servant at Orsino's house?

How did you do?

If you scored 20–30:   You really have read the play and understood it. You're definitely an excellent Shakespearean scholar!

If you scored 10–20:   Not bad, but you need to think about what happened in the play. You missed some things!

If you scored 0–10:   What happened? Were you asleep? You need to go over a lot of the scenes in detail this time!

Stepping stones 1

Look at the game below. It is made of stepping stones that you have to use to get from one side to the other. On each stone are letters and numbers. The letters are the first letters of the words that are answers to the questions on Sheet 2. The numbers are the numbers of the questions.

You have to work your way from one side to the other by answering all the questions on Sheet 2 correctly.

You can start on any stone at the left and move in any direction to the nearest stepping stone. You can double back if you don't know one answer, but to win you have to reach the right hand side.

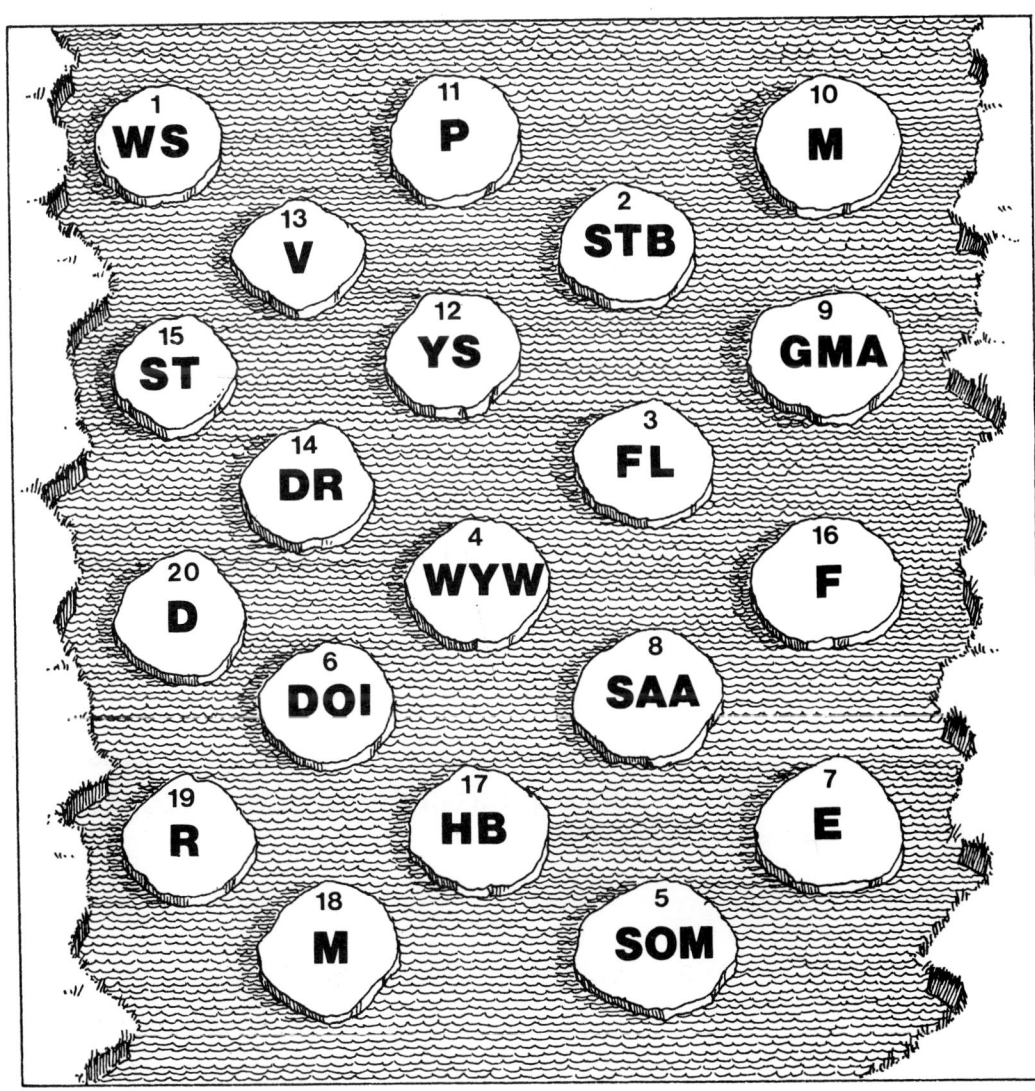

Stepping stones 2

(Continued from Sheet 1)

Questions

1 Who wrote *Twelfth Night?*
2 Who is Olivia's uncle?
3 What did Maria drop on the path to fool Malvolio?
4 What is the other title of *Twelfth Night?*
5 Who is Viola's brother?
6 Who is Orsino?
7 What is the name of the inn where Antonio wanted to meet Sebastian?
8 Who is Sir Toby's friend?
9 What name does Sir Andrew use to Maria when he first meets her?
10 Who does Olivia think is mad when he dresses strangely and smiles all the time?
11 What P does Olivia give to Sebastian?
12 What does Malvolio wear on his legs to impress Olivia?
13 What is Cesario's other name?
14 Where is Malvolio imprisoned?
15 Who does the Clown pretend to be outside the dark room?
16 By what other name is the Clown known?
17 Who has died in Olivia's family and that's why she wears a black veil?
18 Fill in the missing word: 'If M____ be the food of love play on.'
19 What R does Olivia send after Cesario?
20 Fill in the missing word: Sir Andrew challenges Cesario to a D___.

VIP

These three letters stand for **V**ery **I**mportant **P**erson.

There are very important people in your school.

1 On the rungs of the ladder, write down the names of these people. Try to think who you would put at the top of the ladder and who might come after that.

2 When you have done this, share your ideas with a partner.

3 See if you have come up with the same names on the ladder.

The higher up the ladder people come, the higher their **status**.
This means the higher they are, the more important they are.

4 *Twelfth Night* has **very important people**. Using the next ladder, see if you can work out, with a partner, who these might be and in what order they might come.

The first one has been done for you.

ORSINO
Duke of Illyria

Making Malvolio look the fool!

Look at the picture of Malvolio. This shows you an actor who played the part in 1998.

- He has followed the instructions in the letter.
- He is wearing the yellow cross-gartered stockings.
- He is smiling all the time.
- He looks just the opposite of the miserable character Malvolio was before.

No wonder we all think he looks a fool!

Now it's your turn.

Try to draw Malvolio in the costume you would like to see him in.
It has to be close to what the letter says, but you can change lots of things as well, like his hair, his shoes and his belt.
You can colour it in to make it look a lot funnier.

If you can't draw very well, trace the picture of Malvolio on page 25.

Orsino and Olivia

If you think about these two characters, they have lots of similarities – that is, they are like each other in lots of ways.

1 Below you will find some of the ways in which they are alike.

However, these are only points – **you** have to find the evidence from the play that tells you the points are true.

- They both 'go for' the same type of person.
- They both trust Cesario at once.
- They both like to be the centre of attention.
- They both think they know what love is, but to begin with they are only playing at it.
- They are both powerful people, born to wealthy families.
- They both have loyal servants.
- They are both rich so they can spend their time as they want.
- They are both attractive.

2 Can you think of any other points that tell you Orsino and Olivia are like each other?

Designing costumes

Before any play is put on stage, the costumes that the characters will wear have to be talked about.

1 Look at the pictures of Sir Toby, all the way through the comic strip. You can only see him in black and white.

2 Try to decide what colours you might have for his costume.

3 You will need to explain why you have chosen certain colours. For example, if you choose to use a **red** feather in his hat, you might say that that is because he drinks a lot and might have red cheeks and a red nose too!

Remember: the colours and the costume will tell you a lot about Sir Toby's character.

4 When you have done that, share your ideas with a partner.

5 When you have decided exactly what you want, tell the rest of the class and see whether you have come up with the same kind of ideas.

Design your own poster

Below is the poster for a video of *Twelfth Night.*

1 Can you tell who the characters are?
For example, which do you think is Olivia and which is Malvolio?

2 Which characters are **not** shown?

3 Do you think that this design tells you what the film of *Twelfth Night* is about?

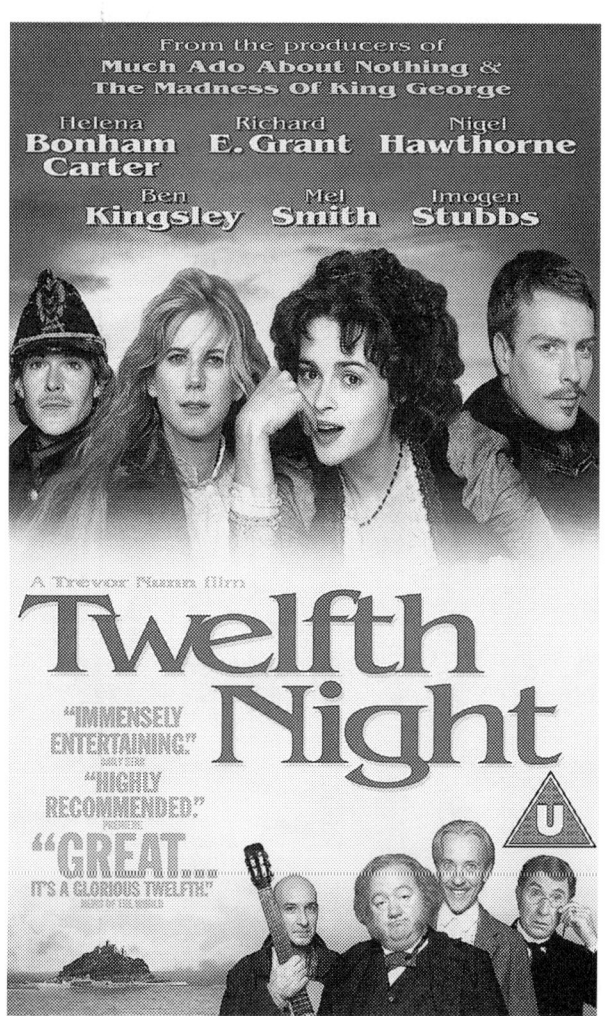

4 Design your own poster for the play.
You could cut pictures out of magazines to show any characters you want. Or you could draw them yourself.

It's amazing!

It's amazing how many people in this play want to marry Olivia!

1 Write their names under the pictures.
2 Draw Olivia's path through the maze to the man she does marry.

Can you fill in the gaps? 1

Twelfth Night really has two stories – the first is to do with Orsino, Olivia, Viola and Sebastian; the second is to do with Sir Toby, Maria, Sir Andrew and Malvolio.

We will call the first story the **main** one and the second, the **secondary** one.

Read the main story of *Twelfth Night* below.

Some words are missing. Try to fill in the blanks. You can use the words underneath the passage, but you can only use each word once.

The _____ of Twelfth Night

The Duke of Orsino thinks he is in _____ with Olivia. He tries to win her love, by sending lots of _____ to her. She will not listen to his messages. When Viola turns up at Orsino's house, disguised as a ___, Orsino sends the boy Cesario to Olivia with more messages. Olivia falls in love with _____. This is no good, because Cesario is really a ___. Luckily Cesario's twin _____ Sebastian did not drown in a shipwreck and he turns up in _____. While walking in Illyria, Olivia sees _____ and thinks he is Cesario. She asks him to _____ her. He is surprised but says yes! When Cesario and Sebastian meet, all the mistakes are put _____. Cesario becomes Viola and marries _____. Orsino is happy now, because he has Viola. Olivia is _____ now, because she has Sebastian.

Words to help you

messages	Sebastian	Illyria	marry	happy	right
story	love	brother	girl	Cesario	boy	Orsino

Can you fill in the gaps? 2

You have already filled in the gaps to make the **main** story make sense.
Now try to fill in the gaps of the **secondary** one.

The secondary _____ of Twelfth Night

Sir Toby is trying to make Sir _____ believe that Olivia will marry him. Sir Andrew is not sure about this. Because he is not very _____, Sir Toby can trick him out of his _____. They use this money to buy _____. When they drink, they get noisy and ____ and _____. This dancing and singing annoys Malvolio. Sir Toby, Sir Andrew and Maria trick _____, by forging a letter, pretending that this _____ has been written by Olivia. Malvolio thinks that Olivia is in love with him and to prove his ____, he dresses up in yellow stockings and smiles all the time. Olivia hates the colour _____ and thinks Malvolio is mad. He is sent to a ____ room. When he is in this dark room, Sir Toby, Sir Andrew, Maria and the Fool tease him. He gets out of the room and is cross when he finds out that the letter was forged. It is Olivia who tells him that the letter was _____. He rushes off shouting he will have revenge. Malvolio is not happy, but Sir Toby and Maria are _____, because they decide to get married. Sir Andrew doesn't get _____ to anyone. He is left to go home at the end.

Words to help you

married	dark	forged	Andrew	Malvolio	money
happy	yellow	letter	sing	love	dance	drink	clever

Invitation to a wedding

The Duke is a VIP – a Very Important Person!
Before he gets married to Viola, he will send out wedding invitations.

1 You have been asked to design one, especially for him. Look at the back cover of the play. That might help you decide how yours might look.

Remember that if you want to invite people to a celebration, you must include:

- the names of the people whose celebration it is
- the date of the celebration
- the time of the celebration
- the place where the celebration is being held
- the names of the people to whom you are sending the invitation
- the address for the answer
- the type of clothes to wear.

You can decide on the size and colour of your invitation. You can also decide on the size of the letters.

2 When you have finished, put your invitation up on the display board alongside everyone else's.
Look at them all and see what they have in common. Look at what is different about them all.
Talk with your teacher about which ones look the most suitable.

Here is the news!

Have you noticed that when famous people get married, there is always a reporter at the wedding who appears on television to tell us what went on?
The reporter gives us a **news bulletin**.

- The Duke Orsino is famous and he marries Viola.
- Olivia is a Countess and she has married Sebastian of Messaline.
- Sir Toby is a knight and he has married Maria, a servant.

These would be worth reporting on the Nine o'clock News.

1 Imagine that you are a news reporter. You are going to give a news bulletin after the Duke's wedding, when they are all celebrating at his house.

2 You will have to plan what you are going to say, by writing down some ideas and perhaps by listening to the news.
Ideas to help you:

- Where will the celebrations take place
- Who will be there?
- What might they be wearing?
- What will the food be like?
- Will there be any alcohol?
- Who might be drunk?
- Who might sing at the celebrations?
- Is there anyone who might be miserable and say something mean and nasty?

3 When you have planned your bulletin, rehearse it by saying it out loud to a partner who will give you her opinion. After that, you can act it out to the rest of your class!

Catching up on the news

Imagine that you haven't seen a brother/sister or another relative for months.
Imagine that you had no idea where they were and suddenly, they turned up safe and sound!
Well, this is what happened to Viola and Sebastian.
I bet they had a lot of catching up to do!

1 In pairs, each take a part: one Viola and the other Sebastian.

You have both got married and you have some spare time to talk about your adventures.

2 Write the conversation that you have. You will want to talk to each other about all that has happened to you both since that awful shipwreck when you both thought that the other one had died!

3 When you have finished, read it out to a small group or to the rest of your class and see what they think.

Remember that you are evaluating your work when you listen to other people's ideas!

Punished or rewarded?

Now that you've finished reading the play, it's your turn to decide whether characters got what they deserved.
Let's think about three characters:

Orsino
He sent messages of love to Olivia. He didn't go to see her himself until the very end. He sat around, listening to music and talking about love all day.
At the end, he got married to Viola. She loved him as soon as she set eyes on him.

Malvolio
He thought he was special. He thought everyone else was beneath him, all except Olivia. He believed that she loved him and wanted to marry him!
At the end, he was locked in a dark room after Maria had made a fool of him and got him to dress up in very silly clothes. Olivia thought he was mad.

Olivia
She said she would see no-one for seven years because her brother had died. As soon as she saw Cesario, she fell in love with him and made a fool of herself by pretending he'd given her a ring. She proposed marriage to somebody she'd only just met!
At the end, she had a good husband to help her run her house. She had Orsino as a brother-in-law and Viola as a sister-in-law.

Imagine that you are a lawyer, like the ones we see on television sometimes presenting their cases to a jury.

Read out the speech you have written about Orsino, Malvolio and Olivia.

You must try to persuade the jury that they either got what they deserved or that they didn't.

At the end of your speech, let the jury decide what **they** think of your case!